KIRSTEN AND THE CHIPPEWA

KIRSTEN · 1854

BY JANET SHAW

ILLUSTRATIONS RENÉE GRAEF

VIGNETTES PHILIP HOOD, SUSAN MCALILEY

THE AMERICAN GIRLS COLLECTION®

Published by Pleasant Company Publications
Previously published in *American Girl*® magazine
Copyright © 2002 by Pleasant Company
For information, address: Book Editor, Pleasant Company Publications,
8400 Fairway Place, P.O. Box 620998, Middleton, WI 53562.

Visit our Web site at **americangirl.com**

Printed in Singapore.
02 03 04 05 06 07 08 09 TWP 10 9 8 7 6 5 4 3 2 1

The American Girls Collection® and logo, American Girls Short Stories,™
the American Girl logo, Kirsten®, and Kirsten Larson®
are trademarks of Pleasant Company.

Library of Congress Cataloging-in-Publication Data

Shaw, Janet Beeler, 1937–
Kirsten and the Chippewa / by Janet Shaw ;
illustrations, Renée Graef ; vignettes, Philip Hood, Susan McAliley.

p. cm. — (The American girls collection)
Summary: In 1856, ten-year-old Kirsten, living with her family
in Minnesota, meets a raiding party of Ojibway Indians
and finds unexpected help when her dog is in danger.

ISBN 1-58485-479-0
[1. Frontier and pioneer life—Minnesota—Fiction. 2. Swedish Americans—Fiction.
3. Ojibway Indians—Fiction. 4. Indians of North America—Minnesota—Fiction.
5. Dogs—Fiction. 6. Immigrants—Fiction. 7. Minnesota—Fiction.]
I. Graef, Renée, ill. II. Hood, Philip, ill. III. McAliley, Susan, ill. IV. Title. V. Series
PZ7.S53423 Ke 2002   [Fic]—dc21   2001036375

The
AMERICAN GIRLS
COLLECTION™

OTHER AMERICAN GIRLS
SHORT STORIES:

FELICITY DISCOVERS A SECRET

JUST JOSEFINA

ADDY STUDIES FREEDOM

SAMANTHA'S BLUE BICYCLE

KIT'S HOME RUN

MOLLY'S A+ PARTNER

PICTURE CREDITS

The following individuals and organizations have generously given
permission to reprint illustrations contained in "Looking Back":
p. 30—© British Museum, London; p. 31—10000.415a-c, Museum Collections,
Minnesota Historical Society; p. 32—Makuk, 10000.25, Museum Collections,
Minnesota Historical Society; p. 33—AV1989.44.284, Artist: Seth Eastman, Minnesota
Historical Society; p. 35—The Field Museum, Chicago, IL, neg. no. CSA 14494;
p. 36—1981.4.32, Museum Collections, Minnesota Historical Society;
p. 37—Smithsonian Institution, Dept. of Anthropology #80-19876;
p. 38—© Smithsonian American Art Museum, Washington, D.C./Art Resource, N.Y.;
p. 39—© Minnesota Office of Tourism Photo; p. 40—Photography by Jamie Young.

TABLE OF CONTENTS

PAPA
*Kirsten's father, who
is sometimes gruff
but always loving.*

MAMA
*Kirsten's mother, who
never loses heart.*

KIRSTEN
*A ten-year-old
who moves with her
family to a new
home on America's
frontier in 1854.*

LARS
*Kirsten's sixteen-year-old
brother, who is
almost a man.*

PETER
*Kirsten's mischievous
brother, who is
seven years old.*

BRITTA
*Kirsten's baby sister,
who is nine months old.*

LISBETH
*Kirsten's thirteen-year-old
cousin.*

ANNA
*Kirsten's nine-year-old
cousin.*

CHIPPEWA OR OJIBWAY?

The Indians who visit Kirsten
and her family in this story are part of
a tribe called the *Ojibway* (oh-JIB-way).
The first white settlers mispronounced
"Ojibway" as "Chippewa," so that
name was used during Kirsten's time.
The tribe is known by either name
today, but most members of the tribe
call themselves "Ojibway."

KIRSTEN AND THE CHIPPEWA

Kirsten stopped scrubbing the soup pot and cocked her head. Yes, she heard icicles dripping—*plink! plonk!*—like notes plucked on a fiddle. "Listen!" she said to her cousins, Lisbeth and Anna. "Icicles are melting! Maybe spring is on the way." How she hoped it was! Then Papa and Uncle Olav could come back from the logging camp, and the Larsons would all be together again. Their little cabin seemed much happier and safer when the fathers were home.

1

"It's just a February thaw," Lisbeth said in her most practical voice. "We've got a long, cold winter ahead."

"I bet it's even colder here than in Sweden, isn't it, Kirsten?" Anna said, handing her a stack of soup bowls. "I bet it's colder in Minnesota than anywhere in the world!"

After supper, everyone in the family had work to do. Anna cleared the dishes from the table, and Kirsten knelt by the bucket of warm water to wash them. As Lisbeth dried the dishes and put them away, Mama stored the leftover food. Aunt Inger had gone back

to her weaving. Seven-year-old Peter's job was to play on the bed with baby Britta. He tickled her tummy and said

2

"Boo!" to make her laugh.

When the food was put away, Mama took
two fragrant dried-apple pies
from the iron stove and set
them on trivets.

"Can I have a piece of pie
now?" Peter said. "Please, please, please!"

"Soon," Mama said with a smile. "Pies
have to cool a bit first."

Suddenly the windows beside the cabin
door went dark, as if night had come early.
Kirsten looked up, then caught her breath
in alarm. Indians! Lots of them! Their faces
filled the windows. Red and black paint
striped their cheeks and foreheads. Their
eyes gleamed. They'd come up to the cabin
without making a sound.

Kirsten climbed quickly to her feet. Caro, who had been lying at her side, laid back his ears and began to bark wildly.

When Peter saw the Indians, he jumped behind Aunt Inger's big loom. "Indians! Why are they looking at us?" he said.

Aunt Inger patted his shoulder. "It's all right, Peter. Indians stop here to trade with us from time to time."

Left alone on the bed, Britta started to wail, and Mama hurried to pick her up. "Indians painted like these are on a raid!" Mama said. She seemed worried, too.

"What's a raid?" Peter asked in a small voice.

"The Indians raid each other's camps to steal horses and supplies," Aunt Inger said.

"Sometimes men are killed in a raid."

"Will they raid us?" Peter asked, pressing himself against Aunt Inger's side.

"No, Peter. They're after other Indians," Aunt Inger said, rising from the bench and beckoning to the fierce-looking men in the windows. "These men are Chippewa. No doubt the Sioux raided their camp, and they're out to get even. The Chippewa and the Sioux have been enemies for longer than anyone can remember. But they've always been friendly to us." She went to the door and opened it.

Kirsten moved closer to her cousins as a few men from the raiding party, their blankets smelling of smoke, filed one by one into the cabin. The men wore headdresses made of animal hair. They had tomahawks tucked into their belts and rifles slung over their arms. Kirsten had never seen Indians dressed as warriors before. She thought these warriors weren't a bit like her gentle friend Singing Bird. If they were after the Sioux, Kirsten was glad that Singing Bird's

people had gone away for the winter!
Kirsten shivered. If only her big brother,
Lars, were home instead of out following
the trap line. If only Papa and Uncle Olav
would walk in the door right now!

Caro crouched low to the floor, his barks
echoing like gunshots off the walls. The
youngest warrior, hardly older than a boy,
scowled at the little dog the way a hawk
eyes its prey. *Will he slash Caro with that long
knife he carries in his belt?* Kirsten wondered
fearfully. She grabbed Caro by his rope
collar and held him tightly. The boy slid
his glance to her, then looked away.

The oldest of the warriors had a long scar
beside his nose and a bigger headdress than
the others. Aunt Inger nodded to him as the

leader. "Hello, Five Swans," she said. "What can we do for you today?"

"Today we hurry," Five Swans said, but he took time to lift the lid of the cheese box and peer in. Another Indian picked up a shiny spoon, pretended to eat from it, and laughed. The youngest warrior's attention came to rest on the two pies cooling on the table. He pointed to the pies and then to the four prairie chickens that hung on his belt.

prairie chicken

"Will you trade?" Five Swans asked Aunt Inger.

"You want pies in trade for birds to roast?" Aunt Inger said. "That's fair."

"Not our pies!" Peter wailed.

"But we need meat, and your mother and

I can make more pies," Aunt Inger assured him. She cut each steaming pie into big sections. "Let me get some plates."

Before she could reach for plates, each Indian scooped up a fat slice in his hand and began to eat hungrily.

"The pies aren't too hot for them!" Anna whispered to Kirsten.

Aunt Inger glanced at the girls. "It's not polite to stand gawking. Don't you have work to finish?"

Anna stepped boldly among the Indians surrounding the table, picked up the empty pie tins, and put them into the wash bucket.

Kirsten tied Caro to the end of the bed. As she knelt to wash the tins, the youngest warrior circled the table to watch her work.

Gobbling down his pie in big bites, he stood close beside her, so close she could see dried blood on the handle of his long knife. *Why is he watching me?* she worried. Nervously, she scrubbed the pie tins over and over.

Then she heard the young warrior say something in his gruff voice to the other men, and they all began to laugh. Kirsten looked up to see the young warrior imitating the way she was washing the tins. He rubbed his hands over and over and spoke again, making the others laugh even harder.

"He calls you *esiban*," Five Swans told Kirsten with a grin. "*Esiban* means raccoon. He says you wash dishes like a raccoon washes its food!"

10

*Kirsten looked up to see the young warrior imitating
the way she was washing the tins.*

Anna and Lisbeth and Peter giggled.
Aunt Inger smiled, and even Mama's lips
turned up.

But Kirsten felt herself blush. In a flash
her fear changed to anger with the young
warrior. He had no business making fun of
her with that stupid name. To hide her
angry blush, she turned to the fire and
stirred it with the poker, feeling her face
blaze like the flames.

"*Esiban!*" the young warrior repeated.

Before she could stop herself, Kirsten
whirled around. "And you're an ugly
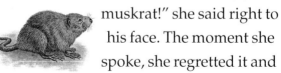 muskrat!" she said right to
his face. The moment she
spoke, she regretted it and
covered her mouth with her hand.

"Kirsten!" Mama said. "Mind your manners!" She looked anxiously at the Indians.

"Don't take offense," Aunt Inger said to Five Swans. "She's just a little girl."

"Little girl who talks too much," Five Swans said. He slapped the young warrior on the shoulder. "She calls you *maanaadiz waajashk!*"

With that, the Indians laughed even harder. The young warrior laughed with the others, but his eyes narrowed. Was he glaring at her? Oh, why had she blurted out that awful name!

The Indians were still chuckling as they filed out into the darkening afternoon. From where he was tied, Caro barked sharply, as though he were chasing them off. Kirsten watched as the Indians ran single file into the woods and quickly disappeared. "They won't stop here again after the raid, will they?" she asked Aunt Inger.

"We never know when we'll see them," Aunt Inger said. "But when they do come back, no more—"

"Name-calling!" Kirsten said before Aunt Inger could finish. "I promise!"

That night as Kirsten crept into bed with her cousins and Peter, she heard eerie howls from the forest. "The wolves are

calling to each other again," she said. She knew they howled back and forth to stay in contact with the pack.

Lisbeth listened a moment to the high-pitched howls. "That *might* be wolves," she said slyly. "Or maybe it's war whoops. The Indians could be camped nearby, doing a war dance around their fire."

"A war dance?" Peter said. "Is that better or worse than wolves?" He pulled the blankets up over his ears.

Anna slipped her hand into Kirsten's. "That young Indian bothered you, didn't he, Kirsten? But your hands did look like little paws, Miss Raccoon!" she said with a giggle.

"That's not funny," Kirsten said miserably. The name still made her prickle, but she wished all over again she hadn't been rude to the Indian. Maybe she'd made him as angry as she'd been. Would he try to get even?

"He was just teasing," Lisbeth said.

"Anyway, I take it back," Anna said. "I was just teasing, too, like Lisbeth was teasing about war whoops. You *were* teasing, weren't you, Lisbeth?"

"I think so," Lisbeth said softly, as if she'd scared herself, too. "Let's go to sleep so morning will come in a hurry."

Anna snuggled against Kirsten's side and squeezed her hand harder. Kirsten squeezed back—she couldn't stay cross at Anna. But she couldn't fall asleep, either. After Mama blew out the candle, the howls seemed to be closer and louder. Tonight their home seemed as small and fragile as a dollhouse standing all alone in the vast dark world.

♥

Kirsten woke the next morning to bright sunshine. The icicles still dripped a silvery patter. After breakfast, Mama handed Kirsten the bucket and shoulder yoke. "Take these to the stream, dear," she said. "If the ice along the shore has melted, you'll be able to dip in a bucket. Maybe we won't have to melt snow for water today."

Happy to breathe the February air without hiding her face in her muffler, Kirsten hurried along the path. Caro, too, seemed glad for the mild weather. He

17

chased a crow and ran back to her with his tail wagging like a flag.

When Kirsten reached the stream, she looked for a place to get water. The ice along the shore hadn't thawed at all. Farther out, where the current was swifter, the ice had melted in patches. But she knew better than to walk out on thawing ice to open water.

As she studied the stream, a rabbit leaped from the bushes and jumped onto the ice, with Caro right on its tail. The rabbit bounded for the middle of the stream, made a swift turn back, and dashed ashore. Caro tried to follow, but the rabbit could turn more quickly than a dog. He lost his footing and tumbled onto his side. Kirsten laughed to see him slipping across the ice. Then she gasped. He was skidding toward the open water! Unable to stop himself, Caro slid off the ice into the deep water and went under.

"Caro," Kirsten cried. "Where are you?"

As she called, he came up a little way downstream. All she could see were his nose, eyes, and the top of his head as he swam against the current. Scrambling, he managed to get his forefeet up on the ice and dug hard at the slippery surface with his nails. But Kirsten saw that he'd never be able to drag himself out of the icy water. It was so cold he'd soon go numb. If she couldn't pull him out quickly, he'd drown. He began to whine pitifully.

"Hang on!" she cried. "I'm coming!"
Without thinking, she stepped onto the ice.
It groaned and creaked under her, and she
leaped back. If she fell in, she could drown,
too! Her heart was pounding. She was
frantic to save Caro, but how?

Maybe he could pull himself up onto
something that wasn't as slippery as ice.

Could he hang on long enough for her to run back and get a board? But he was already losing strength. His whine became a whimper, and fear stabbed her chest. Poor Caro! "Have heart!" she called to him. She began to weep.

Then suddenly, through a blur of tears, she saw figures coming out of the woods. The Chippewa warriors were returning on the path along the stream. Some were running, as before, but now two rode spotted horses. As they came closer, Kirsten saw the youngest warrior was one of the runners, his braids flying out behind him. Five Swans, his shoulder

wrapped in a bloody bandage, rode one of
the horses. The other rider was the man
who'd played with the spoon. He clutched
at his side as if he was wounded, too. The
Sioux hadn't let the raiders get away easily.

Kirsten scrubbed at her tears with her
mittens as the Indians surrounded her.
They all looked at Caro, whimpering and
clawing the ice. The youngest warrior said
something to the others. Was it another
joke, about a dog getting into such
desperate trouble?

No one laughed. Instead, the young
warrior pulled off his moccasins and
leggings. He dropped them on the shore
and stepped barefoot onto the ice. Kirsten
cried aloud as the ice broke beneath his

weight and he sank into water up to his knees. Surely he'd turn back now.

But he didn't. He swung his tomahawk into the ice, chopped a path, and kept wading out. Soon he was almost waist deep in the freezing water. He chopped again and with another step was close enough to reach Caro. Kirsten held her breath as he grasped the dog by the scruff of the neck. He dragged Caro onto the ice, then picked him up. He waded quickly back to shore, where he set the exhausted dog at Kirsten's feet.

Caro shook himself, then began trembling violently. Kirsten yanked off her shawl and rubbed him. "Oh, thank you! Thank you!" she said to the young warrior.

Never in her life had she felt so grateful to anyone. "But you're wet and cold, too! Come to our cabin! Get warm!" She hugged herself and pointed back up the path to show him what she meant.

The young warrior shook his head. He picked up one of his moccasins, held it out to her, and said something in his own language. Kirsten could only make out the word *esiban*. Then he slipped his hand into the moccasin and nodded for her to copy him.

Kirsten hesitated, but did as he asked. Inside the moccasin, the fur lining still held warmth. He was telling her he didn't need help to warm himself again.

The young warrior swiftly put on his

Inside the moccasin, the fur lining still held warmth.
He was telling her he didn't need help to warm himself again.

dry leggings and moccasins and joined the others. Five Swans raised his hand to Kirsten, then motioned for the Indians to move on. With a leap, the youngest warrior ran ahead of the others. He glanced back once before they rounded the bend in the stream and vanished.

Kirsten rubbed Caro with her shawl. "*Esiban*," she whispered, and this time the name made her smile. What name would she give now to the young warrior with the hawklike face? She saw him three ways at the same time. He gobbled pie like any hungry boy. He was a fierce warrior who won horses in a raid. He stepped without hesitation into the icy stream to save her dog from drowning. He was complicated.

She'd call him Three Hawks on One
Branch. If he came back, she'd find a way
to tell him so.

JANET SHAW

At 8   Now

Imagine Kirsten making a bed near the fireplace for wet, shivering Caro. When I was ten, my dog, Timmy, was hit by a car and his leg was broken. After his leg was set, I made a bed for him in a box next to my bed, and I sat with him for hours. Taking care of him made *me* feel better.

Janet Shaw is the author of the Kirsten books in The American Girls Collection.

LOOKING
BACK
1854

A PEEK INTO
THE PAST

OJIBWAY
IN
1854

When Kirsten was growing up, there
were two groups of Indians living on the
Minnesota prairie—the Dakota Sioux and
the Ojibway. *Ojibway* (oh-JIB-way) meant
"those who make pictographs." The name
fit well because the Ojibway kept their
history by painting pictures on birch bark.

When the first white settlers arrived
in the late 1700s, they mispronounced
"Ojibway" as "Chippewa." That name was
used during Kirsten's time and is often still
used today. However, most members of
the tribe refer to themselves as "Ojibway."

*The pictographs
on this scroll tell
a story of the
Ojibway's past.*

The Ojibway were hunters and gatherers who moved from place to place in search of food. They used the phases of the moon to mark time. Each moon phase was named for an event or a type of weather. January was called Cracking Trees Moon, June was Strawberry Moon, and August was Harvest Moon. Each change of season told the Ojibway it was time to move on.

In March, with the Moon of Snow Blindness, the Ojibway moved from their winter hunting grounds to the maple-sugaring grounds. Maple sugar was the main flavoring in Ojibway food, so they needed lots of it.

A cedar bow and arrow used to hunt small game

The women and children tapped the maple trees and collected sap in birch-bark buckets called *makuks*. Then they boiled down the sap into a sugary syrup. To see if it was ready, the women dropped the hot syrup into a wooden mold and set it in snow. If it hardened, it was done. As a special treat, the children got a taste of maple sugar candy.

A makuk

While the women were sugaring, the men fished in freshly thawed streams and gathered materials for building birch-bark canoes. These canoes weighed very little and helped the Ojibway move silently through the water as they fished.

When the Moon of Flowers, or May, came, the Ojibway moved to their permanent homes in the summer villages. These were long lodges that were made with poles and bark. They also had peaked roofs so that heat could rise to the top and more cool air could come inside.

In the summer, the Ojibway tended to their gardens. They planted corn, beans, and squash. While they waited for their crops to ripen, they gathered wild berries, fruits, and herbs. Then they harvested their gardens and preserved the food for the winter.

September was the Moon of Falling Leaves. This was when the Ojibway gathered and harvested wild rice. Harvesting the rice was a festive occasion. Families camped together in small

Men used poles to guide the canoes while women gathered the rice.

groups along the rivers and lakes. They canoed through the marshes and bent the tall stalks of rice over the canoes. Then they beat the seed heads with sticks until the bottoms of the canoes were full of rice. Once the harvest was in, the Ojibway thanked the Creator for the gift and packed makuks full of rice.

In the winter, each Ojibway family moved to its own camp. Families lived in wigwams made of birch bark and moss

layered over a frame of poles. Throughout the winter, the men hunted deer, moose, wolf, fox, and bear. They also tended their trap lines and fished. The women prepared the hides of the animals. In the

A wooden decoy used to attract fish

evenings, the children played games and the adults repaired snowshoes or made new makuks for the maple sugar season.

The Ojibway were peaceful people, but there were times when they were in conflict with other Indian groups. For many years, the Ojibway fought against the Dakota. This happened when the Ojibway tried to gain new hunting grounds that belonged to the Dakota or when the Dakota tried to take over Ojibway territories. Eventually, the Ojibway were successful in driving the Dakota across the Mississippi River.

In the Ojibway culture, children were very important. When a baby was born, the parents

The beadwork on this Ojibway warrior's outfit shows that the owner was an important member of the tribe.

asked an older man or woman to give their child a name. When the child was one month old, family and friends gathered for a special naming ceremony. The elder told them the good things he or she had received from the spirits. These spirits were now being passed from the elder to the child. Then the

Gifts from the elder were hung on the hoop of the baby's cradleboard.

elder announced the child's name, and everyone joined in a feast and prayers for the child's long life.

This ceremonial name was very special to the child. But in daily life, the child used a nickname that symbolized a characteristic or behavior. A girl who scratched her playmates might become known as "Little Cat," or a boy who kept to himself might be called "Stands Alone."

A modern-day Ojibway boy dressed for a ceremony

Today, the Ojibway live on reservations in Minnesota, North Dakota, Michigan, and Wisconsin or in cities across the United States. Many of them are trying to renew their connection to nature and their traditional culture, balancing that way of life with the experiences of modern times.

MAKE BIRDS' NEST PUDDING

A sweet maple treat made with tart apples

When Kirsten was growing up, pioneers harvested and preserved the summer's fruits and vegetables just as the Indians did. Kirsten and her cousins helped Mama and Aunt Inger carefully pack and store the best apples for winter eating and cooking. During the winter, they might have made a special treat like birds' nest pudding. They may have even used sweet maple sugar that they received from the Ojibway. Make this delicious treat for your family and friends.

YOU WILL NEED:

 An adult to help you

Ingredients	**Equipment**
½ teaspoon butter	*2-quart baking dish*
6 tart apples	*Paring knife*
1 cup brown sugar	*Apple corer*
½ teaspoon nutmeg	*Measuring cups*
3 eggs	*Measuring spoons*
1 cup milk	*Mixing bowls*
1 teaspoon maple flavoring	*(1 medium and 1 large)*
1 cup flour	*Fork*
1 teaspoon cream of tartar	*Wooden spoon*
½ teaspoon baking powder	*Sifter*
½ teaspoon salt	*Potholders*
Ice cream or whipped cream	

1. Preheat the oven to 350 degrees.
   Butter the baking dish.

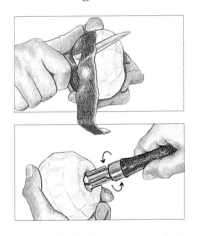

2. Have an adult help you peel the skins
   off the apples with the paring knife.
   Insert the apple corer into the center of
   each apple and twist it to cut around the
   core. Remove the cores from the apples.

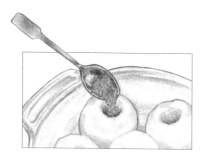

3. Place the apples in the baking dish
   and fill the holes with brown sugar.
   Slightly press the brown sugar into
   the holes. Set aside the remaining
   brown sugar. Sprinkle the nutmeg
   over the top of the apples.

4. Place the baking dish in the oven.
   Let the apples start baking while you
   prepare the batter.

5. Crack the eggs into the medium mixing bowl. Beat the eggs with the fork until foamy. Stir in the milk and maple flavoring.

6. Hold the sifter over the large mixing bowl. Measure the flour, cream of tartar, baking powder, and salt into the sifter. Sift them into the bowl. Stir in the remaining brown sugar.

7. Use the wooden spoon to stir the egg mixture into the dry ingredients.

8. Have an adult remove the baking dish from the hot oven. Pour the batter evenly over and around the apples. Return the baking dish to the oven. Bake the dish for 45 more minutes, or until the crust has browned.

9. Have an adult remove the pudding
   from the oven. Spoon each serving
   onto a plate so the apple is "nested"
   in the crust. Serve warm with ice
   cream or whipped cream.

esiban *(AY-sih-bun)*—raccoon

makuk *(muh-kuhk)*—birch-bark bucket used to collect sap from maple trees or store rice

maanaadiz waajashk *(mah-NAH-diz WAH-jushk)*— ugly muskrat

American Girl®

PO BOX 620497
MIDDLETON WI 53562-0497

American Girl®

Catalogue Request

Join our mailing list! Just drop this card in the mail, call **1-800-845-0005**, or visit our Web site at **americangirl.com**.

Send me a catalogue: Due to a printing error, this card does not meet postal regulations.

Name _____

Address _____

To receive your FREE
American Girl® catalogue,
please call 1-800-845-0005.

City _____ State _____ Zip 1225i

Girl's birth date: _____ / _____ / _____
month   day   year   E-mail _____

_____
Parent's signature